S0-DJW-513

WISDOM *of* PENGUINS

Compiled by
Franchesca Ho Sang

Hylas Publishing®
129 Main Street, Ste. C
Irvington, NY 10533
www.hylaspublishing.com

Copyright © 2006 by Hylas Publishing®
Used under license. All rights reserved.
The moral right of the author has been asserted.

Hylas and the Hylas logo are trademarks of Hylas Publishing, LLC.

All rights reserved under International and Pan-American Copyright Conventions. No part of this publication may be reproduced, stored in a retrieval system, or transmitted in any form or by any means, electronic, mechanical, photocopying, recording or otherwise, without the prior written consent of the copyright holder.

Hylas Publishing
Publisher: Sean Moore
Publishing Director: Karen Prince
Art Director: Gus Yoo
Designer: La Tricia Watford
Editor: Franchesca Ho Sang
Proofreader: Suzanne Lander

ISBN: 1-52958-254-0
ISBN 13/EAN: 978-1592-58254-9

Library of Congress Cataloging-in-Publication Data available upon request.
Printed and bound in Singapore
Distributed in the United States by Publishers Group West
Distributed in Canada by Publishers Group Canada
First American Edition published in 2006

2 4 6 8 10 9 7 5 3 1

WISDOM *of* PENGUINS

Compiled by
Franchesca Ho Sang

www.hylaspublishing.com

"Hold your head **high**,
stick your chest out.
You can make it."

–Jesse Jackson

"We are each of us **angels**
with only one wing,
and we can only fly
by **embracing one another.**"

–Luciano de Crescenzo

“It is **lonely** at the top.”

–Dutch Proverb

"A mother's arms are **made of tenderness** and children sleep soundly in them."

–Victor Hugo

"Be **faithful** in small things,
because it is in them
that your **strength lies.**"

–Mother Teresa

"**Better** to bend than **break.**"

–Scottish proverb

“**Life** takes on
meaning
when you become
motivated, set goals
and **charge after**
them in an
unstoppable
manner.”

–Les Brown

"The **real man** smiles in trouble,
gathers **strength** from distress,

and **grows** brave by reflection."

–Thomas Paine

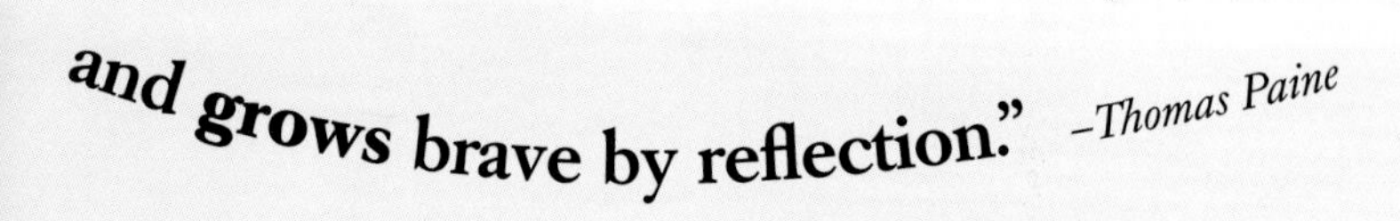

“The **fool shouts** loudly,
thinking to impress the world.”

–Marie de France

"Part of being a winner
is knowing when
enough is enough..."
–Donald Trump

"There are many paths
to the top of a mountain,
but the view is always the same."

–Chinese proverb

“The **most successful** politician is he who says what the people are thinking most often in the **loudest voice.**”

–Theodore Roosevelt

“NO ONE does it alone.”
–Oprah Winfrey

“Every father

should **remember** that

one day his son

will follow his example

instead of his advice.”

–Anonymous

“Only
in quiet
waters
do things
mirror
themselves
undistorted.”

–Hans Margolius

“ People **love** a warm hug,
or just a friendly pat on the back.”

–Maya Angelou

"The arm of the moral
universe is **long**,
but it bends toward justice."

–Martin Luther King Jr.

“Keep **love** in
your heart.
A life without it
is like a
sunless garden
when flowers are dead.”

–Oscar Wilde

"Until you **spread** your wings,
you'll have no idea how
far you can fly."

–Anonymous

“The **footprints** you leave behind

will influence others...” *–Anonymous*

“LOVE IS
the harmony
of two souls singing
together.”

–Gregory JP Godek

"A **true** friend is someone who says nice things behind your back."

–Anonymous

"Individually, we are one drop.

Together, we are an ocean."

–Ryunosuke Satoro

“The man
who has **no**
imagination has
no wings.”

–Muhammad Ali

"Never doubt that a small
group of thoughtful
committed citizens

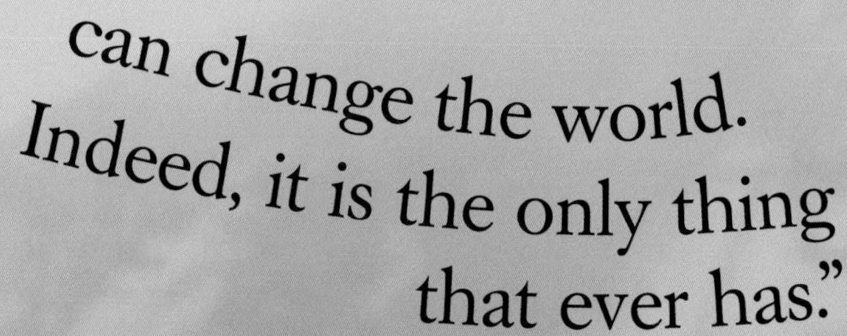

can change the world.
Indeed, it is the only thing
that ever has."

–Margaret Mead

“Leaders
don’t force people to follow–
they invite them on a journey.”

–Charles S. Lauer

“Stolen kisses
are **always** sweetest.”

–Leigh Hunt

“Silence
is the most powerful
scream.”

–Anonymous

“The farther backward you can look, the farther forward you are likely to see.”

–Winston Churchill

"What you leave behind is not
what is engraved in stone monuments,

but what is **woven into the lives of others."**

–Pericles

“Fear is the **lengthened** shadow of **ignorance.**”

–Arnold H. Glasow

"Friends are
as companions
on a journey,
who ought to aid each other
to persevere in the road
to a happier life."

–*Pythagoras*

"It is in the **shelter** of each other
that people live."

–Irish proverb

"Life has taught us that **LOVE** does not consist in gazing at each other

but in looking outward together
in the same direction."

–Antoine de Saint-Exupéry

“Great things

are not done by **impulse,**

but by a series of small things

brought together.”

–Vincent van Gogh

"Never
look down
to test the ground
before taking
your next step;
only he
who keeps his eye
fixed on the far
horizon will find
his right road."

–Dag Hammarskjöld

"If people did not sometimes **do silly things**, nothing intelligent would ever get done."

–Ludwig Wittgenstein

"The best mirror
is an old friend."
–George Herbert

"You are not judged on
the **height** you have **risen**,
but from the **depth** you have climbed."

–Frederick Douglass

“The road to success runs uphill.”

–Willie Davis

“EXCELLENCE
IS NOT A SKILL.
IT IS AN
ATTITUDE.”

–Ralph Marston

"A friend is someone who knows the SONG in your heart

and can **SING** it back to you
when you have forgotten the words."

–Anonymous

“**Never** look down on anybody
unless you’re **helping him up.**”

–Jesse Jackson

“True friends
are those
who lift you up
when your
heart’s wings
forget how
to fly.”

–Anonymous

"For a tree to become **tall** it must

grow **tough** roots among the rocks."

–Friedrich Nietzsche

“Any **fool**
can make things **bigger,**
more complex, and more violent.

It takes a **touch of genius**–
and **a lot** of **courage**
to move in the opposite direction.”

–Albert Einstein

"To **finish** the moment,
to find the journey's end
in every step of the road,
to live the **greatest** number of good hours,
is wisdom."

–Ralph Waldo Emerson

“**Never** bend your head.
Always hold it **high.**
Look the world straight in the eye.”

–Helen Keller

“When rungs were missing, I learned to **jump.**”

–William Warfield

“Of all
the animals,
the boy
is the most
unmanageable.”

–Plato

"Side by side or miles apart,

dear friends are **always**
close to the **heart.**"

–Anonymous

"You gain **strength, courage,** and **confidence** by every experience in which you really stop to look fear in the face."

–Eleanor Roosevelt

"The family is one of nature's **masterpieces."**

–George Santayana

“A dream you dream alone
is **only a dream.**

A dream we **dream together**
is **reality.**"

–John Lennon

“You can stand

TALL

without standing

on someone.”

–Harriet Woods

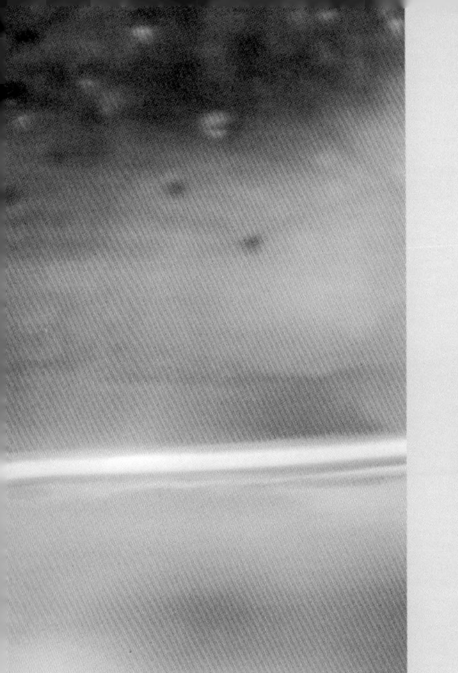

"**Look** beneath
the surface;
let **not** the several
quality of a thing
nor its worth
escape thee."

–Marcus Aurelius

"Nothing ever exists entirely alone;

everything is in relation to everything else."

–Buddha

PICTURE CREDITS

Cover: Photos.com
Front Endpaper: Photos.com
Page iv: Photos.com
Page 8: Photos.com
Page 10: Photos.com
Page 12: Photos.com
Page 15: Photos.com
Page 16: Istockphoto
Page 18: Photos.com
Page 20: Photos.com
Page 22: Indexopen
Page 25: Shutterstock
Page 26: Istockphoto
Page 29: Photos.com
Page 30: Indexopen
Page 32: Photos.com
Page 35: Shutterstock
Page 36: Shutterstock
Page 38: Photos.com
Page 40: Shutterstock
Page 43: Photos.com
Page 44: Photos.com
Page 46: Istockphoto
Page 49: Istockphoto
Page 50: Photos.com
Page 52: Photos.com
Page 54: Shutterstock
Page 56: Photos.com
Page 58: Photos.com
Page 60: Shutterstock
Page 62: Istockphoto
Page 64: Photos.com
Page 66: Photos.com
Page 68: Istockphoto
Page 70: Shutterstock
Page 73: Indexopen
Page 74: Istockphoto
Page 76: Istockphoto
Page 78: Shutterstock
Page 80: Shutterstock
Page 82: Shutterstock
Page 84: Photos.com
Page 86: Photos.com
Page 89: Istockphoto
Page 90: Indexopen
Page 92: Photos.com
Page 94: Photos.com
Page 96: Photos.com
Page 98: Istockphoto
Page 101: Istockphoto
Page 102: Istockphoto
Page 105: Photos.com
Page 107: Shutterstock
Page 108: Istockphoto
Page 110: Photos.com
Page 112: Shutterstock
Page 114: Photos.com
Page 116: Photos.com
Page 118: Indexopen
Page 121: Photos.com
Page 123: Photos.com
Back Endpaper: Photos.com